MINI SAGAS

Creative Capers

TALES FROM THE NORTH

EDITED BY ANGELA FAIRBRACE

First published in Great Britain in 2010 by:

 Young Writers

Remus House
Coltsfoot Drive
Peterborough
PE2 9JX
Telephone: 01733 890066
Website: www.youngwriters.co.uk

FOREWORD

Young Writers was established in 1990 with the aim of encouraging and nurturing writing skills in young people and giving them the opportunity to see their work in print. By helping them to become more confident and expand their creative skills, we hope our young writers will be encouraged to keep writing as they grow.

School pupils nationwide have been exercising their minds to create their very own short stories, Mini Sagas, using no more than fifty words, to be included here in our latest competition, *The Adventure Starts Here* ...

The entries we received showed an impressive level of creativity and imagination, providing an absorbing look into the eager minds of our future authors.

YE CONTENTS OF AUTHORS

Congratulations to all young writers who appear in this book

Hexham Middle School, Hexham

Kelvin Hall School, Hull

Malet Lambert School, Hull

Penwortham Girls' High School, Penwortham

Prestwich Arts College, Manchester

St Aidan's RC Comprehensive School, Sunderland

Shavington High School, Crewe

MINI⚡SAGAS

TICK-TOCK

Tick-tock. The clock seemed to taunt me whilst the seconds passed excruciatingly slowly. The room's tension could've been cut with a knife. I stared at the silhouetted figure standing alert, eyeing me like a fox its prey. I drank in my last moments, savouring them deliciously - the figure advanced.

Emma Carter (12)
Bury Grammar School for Girls, Bury

THE NIGHTMARE

I stumble through the graveyard. My breathing accelerates as I turn around to face my pursuer. I trip and fall. New beads of sweat form across the top of my forehead. My scream fills the eerie silence. I wait for him to kill me. Then I wake up.

Francesca Dack (12)
Bury Grammar School for Girls, Bury

NIGHTMARE

Zoom, it darted through the dark, damp woods. The musty, brown-coloured wolf ran towards me, while I was standing there in surprise. *Crunch, crunch* went the leaves under its feet. I sped off, horrified, as the creepy wolf disappeared into the droopy trees. It was like a bad dream.

Jamie-Lee Kelly (12)

Bury Grammar School for Girls, Bury

THE BLACK SILHOUETTE

There was complete silence. The room was still. The thudding up the stairs got louder. Suddenly, the doorknob started to turn. Thank goodness the door was jammed.
I raced into the wardrobe: I couldn't get in. The door was opening and a black silhouette was standing in the doorway.

India Sawney (12)

Bury Grammar School for Girls, Bury

DEAD MAN'S FOREST

Running faster through the dark frightening forest of the dead man. Cutting down the bushes that got in my way. When out the blue came a king cobra, I didn't see it. *Squish* went the cobra under my foot. Could this be the end for the poor, defenceless cobra?

Eleanor Lewis (12)

Bury Grammar School for Girls, Bury

ON THE RUN

Silence! At last I have shaken off the police. No sirens, no footsteps. Peace. They have been after me for days, no, weeks.
I've been accused of murder and I already have a criminal record.
Oh no! They've spotted me, I'd better sprint away into no-man's-land.

Zara Nawaz (12)

Bury Grammar School for Girls, Bury

THE NIGHTMARE!

I heard a banging noise, so I pulled my cover over my head. I took a quick peek and I was in a place I'd seen before, but where? I started exploring when this man had a knife …
I woke up in a kitchen clutching a knife.

Laura Hudson (12)

Bury Grammar School for Girls, Bury

UNLUCKY TIMES

I was running. If I didn't I wouldn't see tomorrow. 'There you are!' My pursuer shot his gun. It's a good thing he had a bad aim.
I whizzed around the corner and stopped. *Crunch*. I ran behind him and pushed him into the lift shaft. I was finally free!

Isobel Tanner (12)

Bury Grammar School for Girls, Bury

THE BEAST

A blackened sky smirked an electric smile. It roared its gruff, monstrous laugh, causing mighty trees to tremble and faint with fear. The beast's very breath uprooted plants and made creatures of innocence flee. Still, from its eyes fell glittering tears, pounding the earth mercilessly. Was it remorseful? Silence fell.

Charlotte Rhodes (13)

Bury Grammar School for Girls, Bury

THE DARKNESS

I flashed my torch around the room, searching for something that couldn't be found. Suddenly, out of the corner of my eyes, I saw a blurred figure rush past. As I turned my head, something touched me and I heard a trigger. *Click*. A voice called out, 'Any last words?'

Sara Ibrar (13)

Bury Grammar School for Girls, Bury

DEADLY NIGHTSHADE

I walked up to the door. It felt as if my heart was going to stop any minute. Realising that I couldn't do this, I walked away, almost running. Suddenly, I heard a creak. My head automatically turned. There was a strange, shadowy figure behind the door. What was it?

Afsha Sadiq (13)

Bury Grammar School for Girls, Bury

THE RACE OF THE SPIDERWEB

Ready at the corners, like lions pouncing from cages. Loud rings from whistles were heard and we charged at whirlwind speed. Swinging and climbing up the spiderweb, higher into the sunset, like monkeys searching for food. Close to the top, looking back at everyone just below. Could I win?

Rebecca Howard (13)

Bury Grammar School for Girls, Bury

A HAPPY ENDING
TO A SAD LIFE

Slithering, sliding, swerving around, trying to sustain hope, I felt the shot in my head. Bushes became a blur, my senses dulled as I steadied to a halt. Knowingly, I glided onto nearby grass, where I lay happily until the light in my eyes faded and silence penetrated my soul.

Sanya Azam (13)

Bury Grammar School for Girls, Bury

DETENTION

Trembling with fear, I thought about how I got here and why I was here. All these questions made my head spin even more and more. Entering the dark, gloomy room was where the headmistress stood. My heart was beating furiously. I felt my body drop to the floor …

Harshanaa Patel (12)

Bury Grammar School for Girls, Bury

FULL MOON AT MIDNIGHT

The night was dark and the fog thick. I closed my eyes and a hot, moist breath hit my ice-cold cheek. It lingered down the surface of my neck. Cold, sharp fangs penetrated my skin. Thick blood escaped down my neck. I opened my eyes. Was it too late?

Shannon Ryan (13)

Bury Grammar School for Girls, Bury

THE RACE OF RED RUM

I wait in anticipation at the railing. Galloping across the dusty, sandy racecourse, the muscled, groomed horses speed away, ridden by jockeys in their bright costumes.
It's the last forty yards and jockeys tire, horses fall over. After a very close photo finish, the only winner is Red Rum.

Jennie Farnell (13)

Bury Grammar School for Girls, Bury

TICK-TOCK

I walked into the exam room that was deadly silent. Looking around, I saw everyone with expressionless faces. They were frozen with fear.

The smirking teacher handed over the exam papers while we looked at him with fright. The clock was ticking away and my time was running out.

Jemima Meehan (13)

Bury Grammar School for Girls, Bury

DEAR DIARY ...

I fear this may be my last entry. I'm being hunted, by what, I don't know. I feel watched at night, haunted by day. Nowhere is safe anymore ... I am writing this in the dark, scared to turn the light on ... scared of what I'll see ... scared of ...

Hunaiza Ansari (13)

Bury Grammar School for Girls, Bury

LOST FROM THE WORLD

What was that place? How did I get there? Those were the questions I asked myself this time last year. I remember it so clearly because it was the day I became invisible to the eye. Now I am lost from the world and know I will never be found.

Olivia Massey (13)

Bury Grammar School for Girls, Bury

THE SHADOWY FIGURE ...

I walked slowly into the bathroom and it was then that I saw it. The dark, shadowy figure hiding behind the shower curtain.
Slowly, I approached it as my heart was gripped with fear. My mind went blank, I couldn't see. Pain. Silence.

Sarah Buckley (13)

Bury Grammar School for Girls, Bury

UNTIL DEATH DO US PART

He looked at me, shocked, with a tear in his eye. The gun was still clutched to his chest. I looked down at the wound in my side and collapsed, as he ran to me. 'I'm sorry,' he sobbed.
I knew why he'd done it. He loved me too much.

Jericho Taylor (13)

Bury Grammar School for Girls, Bury

MY FIRST COMPETITION

It was almost time for me to race, the pressure that I felt made me nervous. I stood on the diving block waiting for the whistle to blow. Everyone was silent until the whistle went and we crashed in the water. All I could hear was the crowd screaming!

Katie Dell (13)

Bury Grammar School for Girls, Bury

THE SEA

Ducking and diving through the magical, deep blue ocean, amazing creatures foraging for food swim slowly past me. As I dive to the shipwreck of a waterlogged war boat, Jack beside me, I smile as I see a beautiful golden-coloured fish caught in a net beside the crumbling shipwreck.

Imogen Skipper (12)

Bury Grammar School for Girls, Bury

THE BEAST

I swam deep in the ocean, getting away from the roaring beast. Deeper I swam, getting away. I felt brave swimming from a fish's worst enemy - a boat. The boat was getting nearer. My fins and my tail wouldn't cope much longer. I'd done it, I'd escaped from the beast.

Amy Dykins (12)

Bury Grammar School for Girls, Bury

BORN TO KILL

The tension suffocating the air, making it barely possible to breathe. The lioness waits for the thrilling moment to pounce upon her unfortunate victim. Adrenaline runs through her like a white-hot iron rod. She digs her claws deep into the ground and clenches her jaw. Patience is a virtue.

Issy Jenner (12)

Bury Grammar School for Girls, Bury

TOIL, BOIL AND MUSHROOM SOUP!

In the depths of the forest, on a stormy cold night, lived three witches; Shirley, Dreary and Gretel. As the lightning crashed down they began to mix a strand of a horse's hair, a mushroom's head and a fluffy glove. This mixture made a mushroom soup, instead of a potion!

Katie Parton (12)

Bury Grammar School for Girls, Bury

THE BEAUTIFUL LAGOON

In a flash I was there, in the breathtaking lagoon. I was lost for words, the glistening water rushing by. The sun shining brightly on me. I stood by and suddenly, *bang!* I was zoomed back to my plain, boring world. Dreams hold the most magnificent places in the world!

Paige Coulthurst (12)

Bury Grammar School for Girls, Bury

THE JOURNEY HOME

Tom stops, he can hear a whispering sound, it's mumbling something, something familiar.
Tom walks faster, he has the strangest feeling it's following him.
He sees a shadow dart across the path in front. He wonders if he will ever get home.
Tom starts panting, suddenly everything turns into black.

Isabella Clayton (12)

Bury Grammar School for Girls, Bury

FREE-FALLING

Climbing higher, determined to reach the top. Almost there … and then, a rumble, as terrifying as a volcanic eruption. Slowly I slipped away from the canopy, plunging helplessly towards the predator below. My fall, broken by the bough, speared my clothes. I waited for the beast's jaws to snap shut.

Georgina Dalton (12)

Bury Grammar School for Girls, Bury

CONRAD AND ME

Conrad was a little boy I knew. He was really funny and he was my best friend. Unfortunately he had to move. I really didn't want him to, so he decided to move in with me! I was so excited. Now we go to school together and have brilliant fun!

Nikita Harbron (12)

Bury Grammar School for Girls, Bury

IN THE DESERT

In the desert I walked with my friends and we saw an oasis. We were all very thirsty. We got many handfuls and were no longer thirsty. We set off on our camels into the sunset and set off back home. How glad we were to be back at home.

Megan Kirkby (12)

Bury Grammar School for Girls, Bury

THE DISH OF MAGIC GOO

As I stirred the hot steaming dish, a fly came and I swatted it away but my hand accidentally caught the handle and the dish went everywhere. I was so upset. Out popped a mystical creature covered in goo. Its wings flapped and away it flew to the magical land.

Alison Langhorn (12)

Bury Grammar School for Girls, Bury

THE HOLIDAY

Rosie and Charlie went on holiday to Barcelona. They went surfing and a wave crashed over them, forcing them to be pushed to another island. They survived off coconuts and salty sea water. They made friends with the people, and lived there all of their lives.

Hannah Jukes (12)

Bury Grammar School for Girls, Bury

THE HAUNTED FOREST

Faster, faster, I could hear them coming. They were running, trying to catch me. The spirits of the forest, I'd awoken their deep sleep, now they were out to get me. I ran, faster than the wind. Ahead was the clearing, I was almost free. *Bang!* And they were gone.

Kiran Gadiyar (12)

Bury Grammar School for Girls, Bury

UNTITLED

The shadow is lurking around a corner, it's creeping round a bend. It tiptoes down your hallway, hovers above your bed. It breathes its steaming breath on you and then it grabs your bony wrist. You scream and cry for help but the dark, mysterious shadow just really can't resist!

Olivia Cunningham (12)
Bury Grammar School for Girls, Bury

LIGHTNING

There were screams coming from every direction as the lightning was taking its path to Earth. I stood there in shock as everything was happening.
'What can I do?'
I ran as fast as I could to hide.
Lying underneath my bed I cried as I heard my neighbours' screams.

Molly Flynn (12)
Bury Grammar School for Girls, Bury

I TREMBLE

The boat race flashes past, the black one with the roaring engine is the one I see first. The boat has racing stripes and the man driving it is wearing all leathers, like he's riding a motorbike, with sunglasses, even though it's cloudy. It makes me tremble all over.

Grace Johnson (11)

Bury Grammar School for Girls, Bury

JOURNEY TO THE UNDERGROUND SEA

In the ocean I am drowning, everything a blur in my eyes. I see the bubbles faintly rising from my mouth. I see different fish, the clownfish passing by. As I approach the seabed I notice some jellyfish. I try to swim away, but I am frozen, dead.

Ola Johnson (11)

Bury Grammar School for Girls, Bury

THE CHICKEN ADVENTURE

Roger the rooster and Charlie the chicken were trying to escape from Mrs Hickenbottom's pie factory. Their plan consisted of three steps. First step; open the chicken run. Second step; grab some pies. Third step; run.
They failed many times to get out, until the day finally came, they escaped.

Natasha Dutton (12)

Bury Grammar School for Girls, Bury

SOMETHING IN THE MIST

In the picturesque scene the rabbits hopped from field to field, crunching on the crispy dewy grass … A dark, lurid figure started to approach me from the perished and cracked castle beyond. I stopped dead in my tracks as the indistinct creature came closer. Unanticipatingly, it maliciously ripped me apart!

Iqra Shah (12)

Bury Grammar School for Girls, Bury

THE HOUSE OF DOOMED HORROR

It could be heard. She turned round, there was nothing there. She had heard something, she was sure. She turned back around, as cold, dead hands grasped onto her neck and crushed every bone. That was the last of her. She can still be heard screaming in the haunted cellar.

Isobel Clark (12)

Bury Grammar School for Girls, Bury

HUMPTY DUMPTY AND THE GOLDEN JEWEL

Humpty Dumpty went up the hill to fetch a golden jewel. He got to the top, felt tired so he took an afternoon nap. He woke in shock the next day, got back up and fell down again with a bump. His eggshell cracked and the yolk fell out.

Mollie Ingram (12)

Bury Grammar School for Girls, Bury

SHORTENED VERSION OF THE OWL AND THE PUSSYCAT

(Based on 'The Owl And The Pussycat' by Edward Lear)

The owl and pussycat sailed off to sea, for a year and a day. They one day found the Bong Tree land. There they found a pig that sold them a ring for a shilling. Next day they were married by a turkey that lived on a big hill.

Georgina Smethurst (12)

Bury Grammar School for Girls, Bury

PIZZA FEAST

There are many different toppings on a pizza. Traditional tomato and cheese, spicy pepperoni and tropical ham and pineapple. The fresh smell of bread dough signals it's almost baked. Taste buds are ready and saliva flows as the pizza cutter slices the triangles. Hungry eyes search for the biggest piece.

Natalka Sywanyk (11)

Bury Grammar School for Girls, Bury

JURASSIC MODERNITY

Dinosaurs are extinct, yet this one is here right now, snapping and crunching as it leaves a massacre in its wake. Now towards me, the creature runs faster than light, its eyes burning with fire. I hide behind the couch fearing for my life.
Wow! This HD TV is amazing.

Warren Lee (17)

Cheadle & Marple Sixth Form College, Cheadle Hulme

THE KNIFE ASSASSIN

I dived, barely escaping the blade as it fell. My heart raced, blood pounded through my veins. My hands were sweaty as I gripped my own knives. I lunged, aiming the razor-sharp points at my enemy's heart. The screen went blank before they landed.
'Time for bed,' Mum said.

Lily Derrington (18)

Cheadle & Marple Sixth Form College, Cheadle Hulme

THE VICTOR

His blade in hand, he stormed the gate, his eyes aflame with mindless hate. His foe did roar, brandishing scaled fist. He struck, he sliced, but alas, he missed! With a final valiant thrust, the blade pierced the skin and the job had been done. He had defeated his son.

John Farmery (17)

Cheadle & Marple Sixth Form College, Cheadle Hulme

DANGER STRIKES

I heard the waves coming closer. I had only a few minutes till I was swallowed into the deep blue ocean. I felt the cool water round my ankles. I grabbed my towel and bag. I ran faster than ever. I was safe. Never again will I stay that long.

Amy Stevens (14)

Fleetwood Sports College, Fleetwood

THE ATTIC

It banged, boomed and smashed. The attic was no home for a human. Except Roy, who never feared anything, or so he thought. But today was to be his nightmare. The door slammed open, the window smashed closed and in he walked. The suicidal, homicidal dwarf.

Daryll Rankine (14)

Fleetwood Sports College, Fleetwood

IT IS MINE NOW

I stared at my blank paper and chewed my borrowed pen, how was I to write a whole story in fifty words? I tapped the pen on the desk, my hand started to shake, the pen scribbled frantically. I counted the words - fifty! I was never giving this pen back!

Abbie Cooper (14)

Fleetwood Sports College, Fleetwood

SUMMER

It was a hot summer's day so I decided to go to the beach. Firstly I went sunbathing on the sand and I went swimming in the cold water. Then I had a tasty lemonade lolly to cool me down. Soon it started pouring with rain so I went home.

Natalie Knibbs (13)

Fleetwood Sports College, Fleetwood

THE WORLD CUP

The biggest footballing event in the world has arrived in South Africa. England have finished their group top and now they are in the semi-finals. After winning the semi-finals, England have progressed into the World Cup Final, can they repeat the heroics of nineteen sixty-six?

Jack Beane (14)

Fleetwood Sports College, Fleetwood

HERO

One day at home with your family, the next, called out to war, seeing and hearing your friends injured or dying, falling to the floor screaming. Then you go home to see your friends and family, maybe not in person but at least in spirit.

Leigh Andrew (14)

Fleetwood Sports College, Fleetwood

UNTITLED

'Argh!' she screamed, as she woke up to find a spider crawling on her foot. As she jumped up, the spider fell on the floor. She danced around the bedroom trying to dodge the spider then ... *crunch!* She stood on it!

Lauren Chadwick-Greer (14)

Fleetwood Sports College, Fleetwood

DIFFERENT SPORTS

There are many different sports and different styles of sports. There are simple sports and difficult sports, some exhaust you, some do not. Some are fast, some are slow. Some sports use rackets, some do not. Most sports use a ball but all sports are fun, fun, fun!

Liam Anderton

Fleetwood Sports College, Fleetwood

LEO THE PUPPY

I have a dog and his name is Leo. He is a loyal little puppy, he will do anything I say. One day I took him for a walk, we went through the park and then I took him to the beach and he found a dinosaur bone. Wow!

Chloe Tagg (14)

Fleetwood Sports College, Fleetwood

THE SQUIRREL

A squirrel ran into the Pleasure Beach and queued up in the line to get on 'The Big One'. As he got to the top … he got nervous and jumped off. He glided in the air like Superman. Fortunately, he landed in a taxi and went to McDonald's for dinner.

Joshua Garbett (14)

Fleetwood Sports College, Fleetwood

JAMIE BORED IN ENGLISH

Jamie was bored in English. He did no work until Miss nagged him so much and told him to write fifty words. He struggled to do it but after forty-five minutes he got on with it. He was proud of it in the end.

Jamie Murray (13)

Fleetwood Sports College, Fleetwood

UNTITLED

There was a cat called Jim who was bullied by his owner. Every day he woke up to the same routine. One day the cat ran away and didn't come back, and that day, the owner realised how much he loved his cat.

Daniel Turner (14)

Fleetwood Sports College, Fleetwood

DANCING PIG

Porkers, the dancing pig, was rolling around in the mud when he decided to dance for all his friends. They all laughed at him so he cried. But the chicken from the other barn cheered him up by singing. Porkers started to smile and dance some more.

Adam Biggs (14)

Fleetwood Sports College, Fleetwood

DADDY DON'T GO

A boy, girl and parents lived on a street in London. They were all playing and having fun, then the siren went off. The Germans were bombing. So Dad decided to go to war. His wife did not agree but he had to go, so they said their last goodbyes.

Laura Davies (13)

Fleetwood Sports College, Fleetwood

THE CHAIR

There once was a chair used by everyone. Everyone agreed, it was the best chair. Then one day it got robbed by an international chair thief. Everyone was saddened, until they got a couch and everyone was happy … until they got robbed again.

Jack Osborne (14)

Fleetwood Sports College, Fleetwood

THE CIRCUS WAS CALLED OFF!

The circus manager was worried, none of his animals had turned up and the show was about to start. Everyone was nervous and the crowd was getting impatient. Suddenly, the weather turned, the tent pegs came loose and the circus fell down and collapsed on the crowd!

Stephanie Franklin (14)

Fleetwood Sports College, Fleetwood

UNTITLED

Once upon a time there was a beautiful girl who fell in love with a handsome young man. She would look out of her window just to hear his voice. She would let her hair down every night to see if he would come and rescue her!

Laura Impett (14)

Fleetwood Sports College, Fleetwood

UNTITLED

Someone wanted to talk to me so I turned around to face him and suddenly everything went blurred, but this one girl was crystal-clear. She had thick strawberry-blonde hair with sky-blue eyes and skin as white as snow. She was as beautiful as the flowers in summer.

Danielle Thomas (13)

Fleetwood Sports College, Fleetwood

THE RED CAR AND THE BLUE CAR

The red car and the blue car had a race. The red car drove faster than the blue car. The red car turned down the wrong lane, but sadly he ran over a caterpillar. Immediately the red car pulled over. By that time the blue car won the race!

Tom Glass (14)

Fleetwood Sports College, Fleetwood

PREDATOR

It sails on the open water, as the sun shines down on the glistening water. Under the water the predator waits, the small white boat above him. Slicing upward through the water, he hits through the deck. The boat sinks, the predator attacks.
The ocean is quiet. He swims away.

Samantha Eykyn (14)
Fleetwood Sports College, Fleetwood

NERVOUS

On top of the ramp, nervous, shaking, scared. I thought to myself, *£500 prize money.* So I wondered what trick to pull off and … *snap!* I was gone … down the ramp, up the quarter and double back flip and the £500 was mine!

Stuart Snape (14)
Fleetwood Sports College, Fleetwood

STILL WATER

The water was still and quiet, but then the water started bubbling. Something was breathing, something big, very big. The bubbles were getting closer to the dock. Matthew stumbled out his house to see what the noise was and then suddenly a massive whale shot out of the water.

Simon Robinson (13)

Fleetwood Sports College, Fleetwood

UNTITLED

I was dancing, the routine nearly finished. I was thinking, *what if we win! It would be amazing.*
There were four other dance groups. We stood there holding hands, our hearts beating, palms sweating.
They shouted, 'And the winner is ... Royal Funk!'
We were so happy we had won!

Rebekah Phelan (14)

Fleetwood Sports College, Fleetwood

THE HAUNTED HOUSE

As soon as Beth entered the door she got a shiver down her spine. She looked at Lauren and asked, 'Is this place haunted?'
Lauren replied, 'Yes; it's being haunted by Herbert Windsor, he has been here for years.'
When she said that, Beth ran out of the house screaming.

Simon Reddington (15)

Fleetwood Sports College, Fleetwood

WORLD CUP

Waiting in the tunnel, minds racing on what's going to happen within the next ninety minutes?
As they walk out on the pitch the thousands there watching, scream!
The whistle blows, the ball is kicked, teams are fighting to score. Just one mistake is vital. We love the World Cup.

Heather Sharpe (15)

Fleetwood Sports College, Fleetwood

UNTITLED

It started with a few pushes, until the first punch got thrown, stunning the victim. Then it all turned tables when the person who had been hit got the other to the floor and made the crowd gasp with the power of the kick. Then, hell broke out everywhere.

Ryan Thwaites (14)

Fleetwood Sports College, Fleetwood

MOON CHEESE

Since the day I landed on the moon my life hasn't been the same. After taking the sparkly purple moon cheese home the world hasn't tasted anything like it and its magical taste. My dreams have come true; I'm a millionaire and my moon cheese has taken over the world.

Megan Whelan (14)

Fleetwood Sports College, Fleetwood

WORLD CUP FEVER

Rooney and Lampard and Robert Green, all of these are part of England's football team. They have gone to South Africa to win the Cup. The joy they would have if they won the World Cup. All of England behind the team. To get the trophy that shines and gleams.

Jack Smith (13)

Fleetwood Sports College, Fleetwood

THE ESCAPE

All alone, no escape, trembling with fear. Is she alone, or is a ghost here? Running down rickety staircase, being chased with each step. Quick, around the corner, hide. Gasping, breathing, hear the ghost arrive. Catch it in the hairdryer and hope it won't survive! That is, until next time …

Emily Wall (13)

Fleetwood Sports College, Fleetwood

THE MAN WITH THE GUN

Coming home, I saw a man carrying a cigarette and a gun. He went down an alley. I couldn't help myself but follow. He walked and walked. Then he stopped and turned. My heart stopped as he aimed the gun at me. There was silence. Then he shot the bullet ...

Daniel Woolford (13)

Fleetwood Sports College, Fleetwood

A NIGHT IN THE GLOOMY WOODS

He wandered cautiously around the lone, silent, sorrow-filled woods. From the corner of his eye he saw a sharp movement. Was it his crazed mind playing tricks with him? Was it his wild imagination? He couldn't take that risk - he had to investigate further - and so his adventure began.

Connor Gotto (13)

Fleetwood Sports College, Fleetwood

UNTITLED

A little girl lay peacefully on the cool, damp grass. As she gazed up at the night sky, a loud rustling noise came from behind a bush. She jumped and sat up in fright. It all went quiet and then a massive shadow crept over her. Then she was gone!

Sophie Edmondson (13)

Fleetwood Sports College, Fleetwood

THE HAND

The hand touched the ghostly face, soft, gentle. As the day drew to a close, the ghost moved and savagely grasped the boy by the throat, wild and untamed. The attacker disappeared without a trace.
Unaware of where the ghost had gone, the boy turned around and there it stood.

Lucy Hollings (13)

Fleetwood Sports College, Fleetwood

THE ROOM

The door creaked open as he stepped inside, the lights were flickering, the wolves howling. Suddenly, *bang!* The door slammed shut, everything stopped. The wolves stopped howling, the lights stopped flickering. He listened carefully and he thought of nothing, then he heard them again. He opened the door and screamed ...

Ben Longton (13)

Fleetwood Sports College, Fleetwood

THE NOT SO HAPPY ENDING

There once was a prince who wanted a princess that would be faithful, but once he married that princess he couldn't leave her, so he had a competition. He selected two but they were both wanted for fraud. He picked one and they did not live happily ever after.

Harley Horabin (13)

Fleetwood Sports College, Fleetwood

ENGLAND WORLD CUP

The World Cup, we're on our way there, the England squad, so you'd better be aware. Everyone else they don't stand a chance, if we win we will do a song and dance. So grab a beer and watch with a friend, so come on, we're here till the end.

Marcus Wilding (15)

Fleetwood Sports College, Fleetwood

ENGLAND

Here we are, fighting for the Cup, all the nation, wishing them luck. Trying their best to do us proud, performing in front of a chanting crowd. Get in there son, another goal, they keep coming, we're on a roll.

Sophie Pearson (15)

Fleetwood Sports College, Fleetwood

THE NIGHT ELVES

Tall and purple with the longest ears, wielding bows and spears, having no fear. Stealthy in the moonlight but easy targets when it's bright. Beings of nature with elders as trees, watching over them as they run, fight and flee. Druids pray and the marksmen stay, defending their sacred grove.

Andrew Singleton (15)

Fleetwood Sports College, Fleetwood

ENGLAND

England, England, England, we need to sort it out. Forty-four years and still waiting. Wayne Rooney, Steven Gerrard, John Terry, you need to get your game on. We trust in Fabio. The Saint George's flags are out in colour in every house. Bring it home England, come on England.

Thomas Greer (15)

Fleetwood Sports College, Fleetwood

THE CREATURE IN THE DARK

I opened my eyes. Looking back over my shoulder I saw the ebony-shaded creature gazing back at me with frightful crimson eyes. I took a deep painful breath, like a thousand daggers were stabbing into my chest. The ebony creature took one cautious step towards me. It went dark.

Stephanie Hodgson (13)

Fleetwood Sports College, Fleetwood

BEST FRIENDS

The moon's reflection danced in the pond, there a little girl stood, lost and confused. The only thing she had for company was her dog; a beautiful creature built for speed, not fighting. A fierce dog leapt onto Alfie. It was a fight for life. Only one could win.

Charmain Billing (14)

Fleetwood Sports College, Fleetwood

THE FRIGHTENED HORSE!

The horse swept through the strong wind like autumn leaves swaying through the air. She ran through the narrow forest as if she was running from something in the dark. Her feet stuttered as she heard a loud bang behind her. She turned with a frightening stare to her ...

Doreen Kettle

Fleetwood Sports College, Fleetwood

KILLED IN ACTION

The moonlight lit up the night sky, but down below a little old woman cried. Her son went away to fight a war, but just yesterday someone knocked at her door. The man told her gently that her son was killed but fought with bravery.

Andrew Arnold (13)

Fleetwood Sports College, Fleetwood

UNTITLED

As the sun set over the valley, quiet and peaceful everything lay. A crunch of a twig, a rustle of a tree, the nightfall creatures came out to play. Colourful lights emerged from the ground, their wings illuminous as they got ready to fly off into the moonlit sky.

Olivia Birks (13)

Fleetwood Sports College, Fleetwood

PREDATOR

The predator watched his prey through thick bamboo, he moved closer, no sound was made, only the rain falling through the leaves was heard. Then the prey started to get agitated, he heard a sound, he started to gallop away into the moist and damp forest. The chase was on.

Jordan Howard (13)

Fleetwood Sports College, Fleetwood

UNTITLED

In the cold, dark night stood a boy all alone, trembling with fright as a mighty beast stood towering over him. Just as the beast reached out for him a man in black burst out of the shadows and pierced the beast's heart with an arrow, was this the end … ?

Lewis Smith (13)

Fleetwood Sports College, Fleetwood

HILLARD AND THE BEAR

Many years ago, Hillard was walking through a great forest when he heard a noise. A great brown bear appeared in front of the brave warrior and began to charge at him. Hillard then picked up his enchanted bow and shot the beast. It slumped and died. Hillard was victorious.

Harry Laird (13)

Fleetwood Sports College, Fleetwood

UNTITLED

Sir John Macally rode down the forest path and heard a *crash!* He saved a woman from a group of warlocks trying to kill her. They fell in love.
One day, she went into the forest and was killed by a bear. So John decided to strike himself.

Steven Cowell (13)

Fleetwood Sports College, Fleetwood

A LOVER'S REVENGE

The two lovers lived in two towns, towns at war.
One day, news got to him that she had been killed. Grief turned to anger. To claim revenge he assassinated the towns' leaders. His feelings didn't perish. He found her final resting place and took his own poor life.

Reece Brickman (13)

Fleetwood Sports College, Fleetwood

THE REVENGE

The corpse of his son slumped to the ground, snatched by the ravenous jaws of the enemy. Still surrounded by the chaos of war, his father kneeled to join his lifeless son. Grief-stricken, he crashed his blade into the enemy's leg like thunder. *Thud!* Finally, his son was redeemed.

Isabella Hynd (13)

Fleetwood Sports College, Fleetwood

YEAR 13

The peasant stormed in. He believed he was the chosen one. The king of Aragon demanded him to be executed because of his lies.
The execution took place but, just before, the man was lifted to safety by God. He turned everyone against the king. The king was shortly killed.

Liam Fairbanks (13)

Fleetwood Sports College, Fleetwood

GOD OF DEATH

Dreaming of terrifying Shinigami, Yuuki knew she had days to live. Death gods were powerful but she was no warrior. More dreams of Shinigami scrutinising Yuuki's every move.

The final night came with an atmosphere of death. Aware, expectant, she went upstairs. Yuuki suffered a Shinigami death, as a hero.

Shannon Bailey (13)

Fleetwood Sports College, Fleetwood

UNTITLED

Joe heard a scream. He followed it to a crashed ghostly ship. He saw Johnny, a boy he'd shot.

He'd whispered, 'Joe will pay.'

Joe saw his family dead and icy cold. *Crack!* The gun shot. Joe fell to the floor with a thump.

Johnny had got his evil revenge.

Colleen Jones (13)

Fleetwood Sports College, Fleetwood

UNTITLED

Jack was eating lunch. There was a loud thump at the door. Jack got up and answered. No one was there, just a mysterious envelope. Jack opened it. There was a letter and it read, 'I'm coming for you'.
That night the man came. Jack was impaled with a knife.

Stacey Louise Worthington (13)

Fleetwood Sports College, Fleetwood

LITTLE BOY LOST

Tony was adopted, heritage unknown. He tortured his family mentally and physically. His mother despised him and cried in the night, for he killed his father! He could hurt her, but not her children ... he wasn't a guest but an intruder. As she drowned him, she watched with cold eyes.

Josephine Andrews (13)

Fleetwood Sports College, Fleetwood

THE WISH THAT BECAME A NIGHTMARE

Lily spotted a shooting star and made a magical wish. She awoke the following morning to see her wish become a reality. She witnessed a wizard walking away leaving a knight lying alone, lifeless and pale. The spell was too powerful, he was gone for good. It was a nightmare.

Lauren Nolan (13)

Fleetwood Sports College, Fleetwood

THE VISION

One night, sleeping under the stars, Erick the Mighty had a vision, a sibling would betray him for some gold. He woke to find the sibling at his side ... with an axe. He escaped ... this time!
The next night he had the same vision, never to wake ... *again!*

Jack Stote (12)

Fleetwood Sports College, Fleetwood

THAT NIGHT

It was a cold and miserable night. The wind was howling like a whale at sea. She needed to get there quickly; for the meeting. Suddenly, she stopped. Was that a wolf in the shadows? *No can't be.* Then it came out of the shadows. 'Oh it's you!' she exclaimed.

Evie Domingue (12)

Hexham Middle School, Hexham

THE SLEEP OUT

Watching a film in their tent, Josh and Robbie heard a terrifying growl!
'What was that?' whispered Robbie.
Josh peeked outside. It was pitch-black. What caused the menacing growl was now clawing at the tent. They sprinted, shouting, 'Help! Help!'
Nobody answered …

Harry Woods (12)

Hexham Middle School, Hexham

SCREAMS IN THE NIGHT

Lizzie wasn't scared, not yet. She ran along the corridor searching every room. She felt that she was being watched by dozens of eyes. Her heartbeat quickened. The windows in front burst open, curtains billowing. She walked slowly forward, heart pounding. A blood-curdling scream, and she was gone.

Kirsten Murray (12)

Hexham Middle School, Hexham

THE BOY

The boy kicked and screamed, punched, bled, cried. The boy ran, was dragged back, jumped, pulled down, swam, drowned. The boy pleaded and was refused. The boy called and was cut off.
The boy fought for his life. The boy died. The boy awoke, it was time for school.

Hadassah Ezekiel (14)

Kelvin Hall School, Hull

TENSION

Two men face-to-face, the whole world on one man's shoulders. What started weeks ago will be finished by what happens now. Are they ready? One of them is, ready to pull the trigger. The other has no weapons but has an aim. The world holds its breath … *bang!*

Richard Burnett (15)
Kelvin Hall School, Hull

THE MYSTERY OF THE UNDEAD

It is in fact the truth: her body did lie there lifeless to the eye. Blood surrounded her, yet no wound. How was it possible? It's still a mystery. The paramedics came, and after thirty minutes work, announced their last try. And then her body shuddered and she breathed again.

Chantelle Norman-Golding (15)
Kelvin Hall School, Hull

FRIGHT NIGHT

Suddenly, I woke up. My eyes wide open, sat upright, the room was bright like daylight. Then suddenly pitch-black. The clatter of thunder rang in my ears. Peering out of the window, a bedraggled shadow appeared. *Tap, tap.* It howled …
'Open the door, I forgot my key!'
Stupid brother!

Bradley Rudkin (15)
Kelvin Hall School, Hull

RALLY

Standing there in the street, bodies crush me from all sides. People screaming, stale breath rushing past my face. 'Tear it down,' they scream. A sudden roar, the crowd surges forward towards a sleek black Mercedes, government plated. People hammer the windows trying to hit out at them. The BNP.

Josh Ralph (15)
Kelvin Hall School, Hull

LOVE HURTS

Her bright amber eyes sparkled in the demonic light, his evil snarls cursing her. The blade made swift, precise slices, a deep gouge seeping thick rouge. Pain-filled screams ricocheted down the unforgiving cavern, a flamboyant proudness over his masterpiece. He repulsed her but she could not help loving him.

Amy Laverick (15)

Kelvin Hall School, Hull

THE ESCAPE

The mattress creaked under his weight, as he rose from the hard, cold bed. Cautiously, he glanced in all directions, checking he wasn't overheard. Like a phantom he stealthily crept down the corridor, carefully avoiding the squeaky floorboards. Quickly, he dressed, stepping out into the cool autumn breeze. Freedom. *Bang!*

Isaac Pocklington (15)

Kelvin Hall School, Hull

TIME-TRAVELLING CLOWN

Once there was a time-travelling clown. He was really quite stupid. He travelled back to the dinosaur age. The dinosaurs weren't impressed by his jokes. The clown decided to go up to two T-rexes. One took a bite out of him and said, 'He tastes really funny to me.'

Alex Colrein (11)

Kelvin Hall School, Hull

MISS MILLS

The gentle lady standing before me, poised and professional, rarely cracks a joke but always spreads her smile, her intellect is perfect and she'll always go that extra mile. With her red patent shoes she dances around her little room, knowing that she's helped us achieve our hopes and dreams!

Kaylea Hagger (14)

Kelvin Hall School, Hull

FREEDOM

Jumping down from the tree, I hear the rustle of leaves and a stream of sunlight catches my face. My wings unfold and the current of wind takes them. For a moment I soar, weightless, captured by the wind. Frozen in the air. Now I know what freedom is. Heaven.

Lucy Medlam (15)

Kelvin Hall School, Hull

THE CHASE OF A LIFETIME

It was so fast, just like a bullet. Its eyes were blood-red and crazy. I panted and howled as I chased it through the forest. My paws left huge imprints in the mud. The thing turned around to deal a death blow, but I pounced. It screamed in pain.

Rebecca Brown (12)

Kelvin Hall School, Hull

QUAKE

I woke up to a low monotonous hum and quickly realised that I wasn't cold: it was an earthquake. It happened all the time but this was new. The streetlight flickered as it fell, alarming shadows swept through my room. I was too late. I only remember the engulfing darkness.

Calum Barnett (14)

Kelvin Hall School, Hull

UNTITLED

The blood gushes to my head. I slip in and out of consciousness. In and out of darkness. The piercing sound tormenting my eardrums. It's true what they say, my life flashes before my eyes. From birth, to that dreadful moment just a few seconds ago. The moment I die.

Harry Cooper (15)

Kelvin Hall School, Hull

FOREST WALKER

There the deer stood in the clearing. He'd been tracking this one for a while. He held up his rifle, aimed, took a deep breath … The deer fell onto the grass. It had been clean and painless. Now the forest walker had food for the family. He turned and departed.

Connor O'Neill (15)

Kelvin Hall School, Hull

THE FIFTY WORD STORY

He ran from the creature, blood pouring from its mouth. It pounced. His head came off in a clean rip. He laid there, decapitated, his head by his hand. The creature tracked its next victim down a dark alley. There was a blood-curdling scream. Total number of dead - 10!

Phillip Baker (15)

Kelvin Hall School, Hull

THE FINAL

This was it. The men came face to face in the ring. The whole world had waited for this moment to come. They stared at each other, eyes glaring into the opponent's. They were instantly focused. No one was going to get in the way. The bell rung and *bang!*

Chris Clark (14)

Kelvin Hall School, Hull

BEST MAN

The room fell silent. Beads of sweat dripping from my forehead. I tried to stand but my knees felt weak. I collapsed back into my chair. All eyes were on me. I plucked the courage and strength to stand. I walked up to the lonely stage. I began to speak.

Daniel Dispenza (15)

Kelvin Hall School, Hull

THE OBJECT

And then she saw it. The small, smooth, round object, glinting in the blazing sun. She moved closer, taking in all the details. The bluish-silver hue, the ornate Celtic pattern, carved delicately into the surface. She reached out to touch it, but it was gone, vanished into a dream.

Jessica Whitfield (14)

Kelvin Hall School, Hull

MISSED OPPORTUNITIES

Tom was a drummer in a local band who dreamt of being a star. Two local buskers formed a band, 'The Housemartins', and invited Tom to join them, he turned them down and his life slowly fell apart. They're millionaires. He's a divorced alcoholic.
Take life's chances when they appear.

Jenn Wilson (15)

Kelvin Hall School, Hull

ENTERTAINMENT FROM ANOTHER ERA

Clang of metal upon metal rings deep into darkness. Jeering crowds pressing in. Flashing sword falling hard against his oiled shoulder, severing sinew, sending hot blood gushing down his arm. Ignoring the pain, launching one final attack. His opponent's head rolls. Slowly turning to face the emperor, sentenced to death.

Kelly McRae (15)

Kelvin Hall School, Hull

WAITING

The man waited in the darkness. His eyes glittering like sapphires in the moonlight. The wind danced through his dark hair, shadowing his pale complexion. A figure stumbled suddenly out of the gloom and handed him a piece of paper. Alone again, he unfurled it. It contained one word: 'Boo!'

Kiah Murray (15)

Kelvin Hall School, Hull

ROOM 36

I moved swiftly down the stairs; my breathing became quicker and heavier as I reached the bottom. The lights in the long corridor flickered as I began to run down it. Looking at every door number as I ran, I spotted it. Number 36. I steadied my breath, reached forward …

Dean Wheldale (15)

Kelvin Hall School, Hull

THE GRUDGE IS COMING TO GET YOU!

'This film is fantastically terrifying, let's watch it.'
'I'm getting a bit freaked out.'
Slam! The door slams.
'Nothing's there!'
The two girls go to the door. 'Argh.'
A little girl with her hair covering one eye stands there with her head at her side.
Slash!
'Argh!'
Terrified, they drop.

Harry Bryan (13)

Kelvin Hall School, Hull

TWO SEPARATE LIVES

Bella and Jacob had two separate lives and lived alone. They saw each other for the first time and felt love at first sight. What Bella did not know, was that he was a frightening werewolf. Bella was in danger all the time. The day came. Bella suffered in silence …

Ellie Jade Shortman (13)

Kelvin Hall School, Hull

UNTITLED

A single teardrop said more than a thousand words had failed to say. She swept it aside and took a breath. The words flowed out of her mouth with no denial. Whole-heartedly and true, I had waited all my life to hear them. The waiting over: 'I love you.'

James Fenny (15)

Kelvin Hall School, Hull

UNTITLED

Tiny, fragile bones peeping through her pale, delicate skin, she's been here before. Her own reflection repulses her. Skin and bone and nothing else. She's making herself weak, killing herself. She fails to realise this. Tears of pearl run down her face. She remains seeking a distorted version of perfection.

Eve Rouse (15)

Kelvin Hall School, Hull

THE NIGHT WATCHER

They walked slowly down the dark alley, their path illuminated by the ghostly moon. Footsteps clicked in the distance and their pace instinctively quickened. Knowing they were being followed, they took each other's hand and, as the stormy clouds burst like an old, rusty pipe, they ventured into the unknown.

Lydia Edwards (15)

Kelvin Hall School, Hull

THE MYSTERY

In a so-called haunted city an abandoned slave came in pity. He was so terribly bad his prince got so mad. He followed him until midnight and then the slave saw a knight all haunted black with red glowing eyes and a lance in his hand. Another person dies!

Ethan-Kai Harland (11)

Kelvin Hall School, Hull

UNTITLED

As I moved into the old, abandoned mansion, I was immediately met by the steps infested with cobwebs and cracks. I began to make my way up and, after reaching the top, a tall dark figure approached me, I quickly stepped back. He suddenly stopped, and reached for his gun ...

Toby Costa (15)

Kelvin Hall School, Hull

UNTITLED

Lying in bed, I hear the crash of thunder whilst the lightning illuminates my room. Hands by my side, I dare not move even an inch in case he hears. I slowly move towards my door as quietly as possible. Suddenly, the door flies open. He sees me, then shoots!

Lucy Waudby (15)

Kelvin Hall School, Hull

MIDNIGHT MADNESS!

A gang of teenagers were walking in a dark forest at around about midnight, finding somewhere to put their tent for the night.

As a shadow passed the tent it began to shake repeatedly, they started to panic. One of the gang members shouted, 'Who's there?' But *no* reply.

Sammie Wray (13)

Kelvin Hall School, Hull

HOW?

Waking, with the desolated breeze rising up in my weak body, I manage to pull my weight up from an old bench at the back of an isolated church. The stench of alcohol is engraved in my body, as I am stumbling down the empty chapel. How did this happen?

Lydia Templeman (13)

Kelvin Hall School, Hull

DRIPPING BLOOD

Julie jumped out of bed. She heard names being called. As she walked out of the door a man grabbed her. He had a sharp knife and put it to her neck. Then a minute later blood was dripping from the knife, but Julie was safe, sleeping in her bed.

Lauren Schofield (13)

Kelvin Hall School, Hull

FISHERS' SURPRISE

I went to Fishers Park with Keeley. As we got there we saw a man watching Keeley's distant cousin. Suddenly, he jumped at her and pulled out a knife. Keeley, without thinking, jumped out to save her cousin. Seconds later a woman came running with 999 typed in her phone.

Bethany-Jo Logan (12)
Kelvin Hall School, Hull

CAN YOU HEAL MY HEART?

I could feel my heart thumping as I ran. The blood was rushing through my body. I felt heartbreak and loss of trust in Toby, in Sam, in everyone. I kept running and running but where? It felt like I was running into endless roads of darkness and loneliness forever!

Megan O'Brien (12)
Kelvin Hall School, Hull

MURDER MYSTERY

I was in my room. There was a shadow. The shadow moved across my flowered room. The shadow grew closer, closer. I opened my mouth and screamed, sort of excited, but silence was in the room. It stood, waiting, in front of me. 12 struck the clock. I was dead ...

Mollie Allison (13)

Kelvin Hall School, Hull

WHEN DARKNESS FALLS

One day, some friends got bored. They decided to go out at night. When they did it turned into Hell. The nearby cemetery was the place to go. Something moved really quickly and before they knew it their friend Bob was dead. Scared and frightened they all ran away hurriedly.

Josh Blades (13)

Kelvin Hall School, Hull

UNTITLED

A dark alleyway and something lives there, no one knows what it is.

I turned around and saw something move. I said, 'Hello, anyone there?'

Then whatever it was replied, 'Argh! Help me, I need food.'

So I walked slowly to the end of the alleyway and saw zombies ...

Ryan Edwards

Kelvin Hall School, Hull

THE DARK FOREST

Clambering through the forest, being pursued by a bloodthirsty axeman, as I managed to escape his claws of death.

It was a cold, dark night and a full moon was risen, all was quiet apart from the disturbances from the unlucky soul who walked across his bloody path.

George Newby (14)

Kelvin Hall School, Hull

THE EERIE INVITE

Swaying in the cool midnight breeze, it is eerily inviting me in. Should I turn back? My heart is going *boom, bang, boom* as I sprint towards the haunted mansion I'm in. The floorboards creak as I tiptoe across them. Suddenly, the door slams behind me. I am not safe …

Charlotte Pickering (14)
Kelvin Hall School, Hull

I DON'T KNOW

The noise was getting louder, the smell was getting stronger and the light was getting lighter. There was a scream. Then another. Then I saw it. There was, a huge purple hippo charging towards us, wide-mouthed, blood dripping, hungry for flesh. Ready for the taste of fresh human flesh …

Chris Wilson (13)
Kelvin Hall School, Hull

THE MAN WHO LIVED IN A SHOE ...

A man lived in a shoe. Now, this shoe didn't smell very nice so the man decided to move. He went in search of his new home, finding a red mushroom tree which was far too tall, and a magic wonderland with a talking cat. So he moved to Morocco.

Sophie Chapman (14)

Kelvin Hall School, Hull

MARIO

I jump, dodge as red fireballs fly all around me. Below me a flimsy wooden bridge rocks to and fro, above a glowing river of molten red lava. I jump over my foe and grab the hammer. The bridge shatters. A toad exclaims, 'Mario, your princess is in another castle.'

Jack Dewhirst (14)

Kelvin Hall School, Hull

DREAMS DO COME TRUE!

The beat of the music spoke to me, it made my heart go boom and my feet eager to get up and dance - but then I realised it was all a fantasy and that it would never become reality.
Then suddenly the phone rang - it was the dance school calling!

Lewis Turner (14)

Kelvin Hall School, Hull

SUN

The sun shone down on the happy scene. Two young lovers, laughing in the sun. Her smile outshone the bright light. His soft voice silenced the singing birds so as to hear him better. The perfect picture of happiness. *Bang. Scream.* She fell. So did his tears. Then nothing. Black.

Carys Thomas-Osborne (14)

Kelvin Hall School, Hull

UNTITLED

The ruthless knife thrust a clean cut in my side. I couldn't move. Blood was draining from my mangled body. He came at me with his vengeful knife again. My pain was minimal. I felt only a tugging every time he removed his devoted friend. My soul left this world.

Megan Long (14)

Kelvin Hall School, Hull

LUCKY

Something stirred in the shadows. I stopped, squinting into the darkness of the alleyway. Images flew through my mind; a murderer, an escaped criminal, armed with a knife or gun. I stood still, petrified, immobilised, barely daring to breathe.
Suddenly, a light flickered on, revealing a cat skulking silently away.

Bridie Edwards-Mowforth (14)

Kelvin Hall School, Hull

A SOLITARY STAR

It was a dark night. The kind of pitch-blackness that engulfed you as soon as you closed the front door. That indigo-blue front door that was the threshold for so many memories … but now was not the time. I focused straight ahead on a solitary star and jumped.

Olivia Dawson (14)

Kelvin Hall School, Hull

OH SO COLD

He folded his shirt, making sure the sleeves weren't untucked, and put it away in his closet. He sat down in his old worn out armchair. Then he picked up the gun from the table next to him, placed the hard, cold metal against his head, and pulled the trigger.

Rachel Innes (14)

Kelvin Hall School, Hull

SHIVER

It was dark, smells of night filled the air. Cat-like, she walked away. Safe now. But, oh! His breath touched the back of her neck. Her spine stiffened. His fingers brushed her skin, soft as a whisper. She turned. His eyes shone. 'Don't worry, it's over now.' She nodded.

Abigail Winn (14)
Kelvin Hall School, Hull

THE PAPER WAIT

I sit, I wait for the moment to arrive, the sound of the clock is deafening in the silence. How much longer will I have to wait? The anticipation is too much, but wait is all I can do. *Thud!* It's here! My evening addition of the Hull Daily Mail!

Chloe Beverley (15)
Kelvin Hall School, Hull

THE SMART CAR ATTEMPT AT MURDER!

'Are we there yet?' I repeated. Travelling in my mum's new Smart car was so boring, until my mum crashed into someone at 20mph. It was my dad. She wanted revenge on him for getting them a divorce.
The next day at court, she was found guilty of attempted murder.

Jordan Colrein (15)
Kelvin Hall School, Hull

FADING BREATH

Fingers brushed his soft, pale face. Lying, 'fragile' labelled across his heart. Breath too slow to count, a beeping machine keeping track of his lifeline.
Cough, splutter. The racing of emotion and doctors. Silence.
Beep, beep. Too fragile to touch, too powerless to fight. Have to watch, my withering love.

Jasmin Harbord (15)
Kelvin Hall School, Hull

THE HOT HEAT

As the burning ground tingled on my feet it felt like a volcano erupting on the tip of my toes. As I opened my eyes a hot red gush of air went past. My eyes began to water. I was so confused. I thought I was safe. I guess not.

Chloe Stephenson (15)

Kelvin Hall School, Hull

MYSTERY FIGURE

The tall, dark stranger swam swiftly into the dark, cold water, its eyes searching all around, as if it was waiting for something to come towards it.
Snap! Something dragged it down.
The dark figure began to throw its arms back and forth, until it came to a stop.

Abigail Pearson (15)

Kelvin Hall School, Hull

UNTITLED

There once was a lion called Bruce. He was the strongest, scariest lion in all of the land. But on one fine day; whilst Bruce was lounging in the hot midday sun, a man like no other man dared to battle the fierce lion. His name was Chuck Norris.

Allannah Harraway (13)

Kelvin Hall School, Hull

THE IMPOSSIBLE CHOICE

The moonlight shone on her dark lips, tension growing between them. One must shoot, one must die. The impossible choice, lose her love or lose her life. She raised her gun, but could not shoot. Her tears pooled around her, and she made the impossible choice .... She lost her life.

Peter Goodwin (13)

Kelvin Hall School, Hull

RETURNING HOME

She hadn't been since she was a girl, so she quickly ran down the lane to see a glimpse of the house she had once called home. Her excitement built as she rounded the corner; only for it to plummet when she saw nothing but a deserted patch of land.

Jennifer Railton (15)

Kelvin Hall School, Hull

HE IS AN INTERESTING FELLOW

My monkey, he was an interesting fellow. He lived in a jar of mustard, although he hates mustard. It turned him yellow. He always carried a tub of pancake mixture. He wore a green poncho and a sombrero made of Doritos. Like I said, 'My monkey he's an interesting fellow.'

Jack Booth (15)

Kelvin Hall School, Hull

HALLOWEEN NIGHT!

He was coming for me, with his pale face and dead, hollow, black eyes. His blue lips, frightful scars, the agitated twitch of his crooked neck meant one thing! Everyone told me he'd died, but I didn't believe it, until then. I screamed, petrified. He laughed. 'Happy Halloween!' he sang.

Lisa Sutherland (14)

Kelvin Hall School, Hull

THE CAVE

It just kept on going and going, stretching away into the blackness. Already the entrance was only a speck of light far in the distance. Not many people go down anymore into the sinking depths but even fewer come back up. A few get lost but there are other reasons.

Matthew Legard (15)

Kelvin Hall School, Hull

NEW YORK MORNING

I sigh, feeling the breeze up my arms on the Brooklyn Bridge. Something good, almost willing me to turn around. The ocean beneath me dances and twirls like a glowing portal to another new life. I hear the sirens and a squeal of wheels, and without a thought, I jump.

Emma Smith (15)

Kelvin Hall School, Hull

I'M NOT GONNA WIN

When it came down to writing this story, my mind went blank. Went into a daydream, just like usual. Why did Miss make me write this story? I'm rubbish at English. Just wanna throw this in the bin. Seriously, have you read the competition, it's not like I'm gonna win.

Luke Robinson (14)

Kelvin Hall School, Hull

THE LIFE OF A SECRET NINJA!

Swimming in the sea, out of nowhere a psycho penguin attacks. It pecks my arm and I start to bleed. Then I unleash my secret ninja move and slice it into a thousand pieces. Good job I went to the secret ninja school in the south of the Atlantic Ocean.

Masimba Matongo (14)

Kelvin Hall School, Hull

WHISPERS OF THE NIGHT

Followed down the alleyway. Strike to the head, slit to the throat. It's over. Last breath. Last drop of blood on the damp floor, last deserting beat of an unloving heart. The unloved gone, abolished from the world. The night shocked to silence, teased away the last whisper of evil.

Izzie Glazzard (13)

Kelvin Hall School, Hull

BORIS AND HIS SCARE ...

The lack of light in the tunnel faded, and Boris left in darkness. He could feel something towering over him, its breath encasing his face. Boris backed and felt the cold bars of a metal cage; he was trapped! The lights flashed on and Boris looked up. A bloody giraffe!

Megan O'Hara (14)

Kelvin Hall School, Hull

ROSES OF BLOOD

I never understood the meanings of flowers, but they still all meant something to me. From passionate reds of roses to the deep violet of tulips, seeming to capture your soul. They'd always been my secret, my garden behind the hill, but today was unlike always, I was not alone ...

Hannah Palmer (13)

Kelvin Hall School, Hull

IT'S THERE

My breath turns white as it hits the coldness, my face turns as pale as snow. It's there, haunting me, all around me. *Thud!* What was that? I'm seeing things I never thought were possible. I swipe blue bottles from my jacket. Spacious spaces start to close up ... What's wrong?

Kelly Jayne Gale (12)

Malet Lambert School, Hull

ALL ALONE

Everything went dark. Chills climbed up my spine. The hair on the back of my neck stood on end. A musty smell hung in the air. I could tell from the silence I was alone. I recognized the smell. Blood. I felt what seemed body-like. It was cold, dead.

Harriet Gornall (13)

Penwortham Girls' High School, Penwortham

THE CHASE

I ran through gnarled branches using my remaining energy. Wolves howled behind as their paws thumped on the damp forest floor. The large crystal-like jewel slipped from my palms, as I was filled with terror. I sensed a dead end, rooted to the spot, horror consumed me. Then death.

Fatima Harlock (12)

Penwortham Girls' High School, Penwortham

JUMPY LUMPY

Jumpy Lumpy sat on a fence. Jumpy Lumpy found a two pence, he reached for the coin and made a big dive and therefore landed in a beehive. Jumpy Lumpy was in a lot of pain, it also ended the day with lots and lots of rain!

Hafsah Bargit (13)

Penwortham Girls' High School, Penwortham

THE FEAR OF DETENTION

'Kill me!' I beg. The deed was done, it was too late, there was no going back! The regret I felt. The nerves eating me away, my stomach churned awkwardly. My palms all moist, my body shook violently. Darkness took over! Today, the day I receive my very first detention!

Abbie Kitcher (13)

Penwortham Girls' High School, Penwortham

DREADING

The air was cold. The wind whipped me as I shivered. I couldn't go … rain lashed down and drenched me. I inhaled and stepped forwards. My heart was thumping in terror. How I wished I'd stayed behind. Now I was alone I couldn't go on! I couldn't go to school!

Aamina Desai (12)

Penwortham Girls' High School, Penwortham

TOO CLOSE FOR COMFORT

The grey bulge stood strong. It wouldn't move, not until we did. A snort of pent up fury made us jump out of our tense state. One move of its huge, bulky foot increased to rapid stomping, by this time we had set off sprinting for the truck ...

Hannah Whalley (13)

Penwortham Girls' High School, Penwortham

A MOMENT

The moon watched on. The soft breeze an embrace. The stars the twinkle in a lover's eye. A raven's bitter song halted silence's attack. Longing and hunger beat my heart. Loneliness beat my wings. The wind strengthened, twisting my hair and dress as one. I raised my wings and flew.

Georgia Clarke (13)

Penwortham Girls' High School, Penwortham

THE SAD TRUTH

I loved him as soon as I saw him. His hair flopped lazily over pale skin. His green eyes glistened in the sun. He smiled, I melted like butter. We were meant for each other. He looked at me, and all he said was: 'What you looking at you idiot?'

Megan Lund (13)

Penwortham Girls' High School, Penwortham

DEATH BY THE CLOAKED DEMONS

I was entrapped by the cold. Cloaked strangers with blood-red eyes, peering at me like dinner. They whispered, they leaned in towards me, hunger in their eyes. They opened their mouths, snarling. Sweet cool breath wafting into my senses, he bit me, venom spreading into my blood. Death!

Jenny Higham (13)

Penwortham Girls' High School, Penwortham

THE PRICE OF LOYALTY

'Kathy … Kathy? Hmph! I'll find you myself then!' grumbled Sophia, storming up to the house and flinging open the door.

She tramped up the stairs and found that the only prize for her loyalty was a pool of crimson blood … and the echo of footsteps down the corridor behind her …

Ella Holden (13)

Penwortham Girls' High School, Penwortham

FALLEN

Fast-moving limbs dragged me to the moss-covered cliffs, the jagged edges made me hesitate, but I overcame, stumbling upon a steep and stony ending. The beastly terror was approaching, his footsteps louder. But I wouldn't hail, my stubbornness had led me here, therefore, inching back, I greeted Death.

Sana Bux (12)

Penwortham Girls' High School, Penwortham

THE PLUMMET

The anticipation was killing me. The Earth grew. The engines roared like a hungry lion, but I was silent, fear swallowed me. The engines cut off. The door opened. I couldn't, but I had to. I jumped. I plummeted. The ground approached. I pulled the cord. Cord? I was gone.

Ashleigh Brooks (13)

Penwortham Girls' High School, Penwortham

THE FALL

The wind slapped against her face, pushing her blonde ringlets behind her. She knew it was coming, she knew she was going to fall.
She took a step, all doubt went. Hope had appeared. Maybe God decided to give her another day. Flowing tears stopped, but suddenly she fell. *Death.*

Ayesha Bux (13)

Penwortham Girls' High School, Penwortham

WHEN THE SUN GOES DOWN

Reach into the dark. Take out my heart. Suck the blood of life. Bite me alive. Rip off my head. Glare into my soul. I shrivel inside. Spiritually dead. You walk away. Cover your face. Close the door. The room is silent. I cover my mouth. Gasp. I am dead.

Katie Lee (13)

Penwortham Girls' High School, Penwortham

TWILIGHT NEW MOON

She ran for her life, the black wolf growling behind her. Jacob Black jumped over the fence.
'Jake, run, it's Paul, he's the wolf!'
He ran towards her, then leaped over her and transformed into a brown wolf. Jake was a wolf. Astounded, Bella watched the two beasts fight fiercely.

Sara Aslam (12)

Prestwich Arts College, Manchester

CARGO SHIPS MAKE MONEY

Money, money, money, all anyone ever thinks about. Money makes the world go round. Cargo ships make money. Not this one though.
I set the dial to thirty seconds, jumped off the boat and inevitably waited for the explosion. If it was up to me, there wouldn't be any money.

Callum Stringer (13)

Prestwich Arts College, Manchester

THE UNKNOWN BODY

It's one in the morning and I can't sleep. Suddenly, I notice a shadow of a person dragging a small body behind it. I know that it is coming into my room; it comes nearer and enters.
'I can't sleep,' says my little brother, dragging his teddy bear behind him.

Roohi Khushtar (13)

Prestwich Arts College, Manchester

THE LONELY BOY

Another day for Charles. He walks straight past children, but nobody speaks to him. He walks through a football pitch, nobody speaks to him. He walks and cries through streets, but nobody looks. He walks into the road and gets hit by cars and carries on walking, still crying.

Kane Sheldon (13)

Prestwich Arts College, Manchester

FREAKED OUT!

He ran as fast as he could, but it was no use trying - it was right there - he could feel it right behind him. He tried to yell for help but nothing came out. He was trapped in his nightmare, alone, afraid. The bully had caught him.

Adam Walsh (13)

Prestwich Arts College, Manchester

THE FOREST

A family were on their way home, when they took a short cut through the forest ... After a while their car battery went. They got out the car, there was no signal on the mobile. They had to walk.

One of them disappeared into the dark. You could hear screams ...

Umar Mushtaq (13)

Prestwich Arts College, Manchester

13

I saw her running through the woods, scared. Long, straggly hair flew behind her. Her ragged clothes and bloodshot eyes and the blood on her hands. I soon awoke from the terrible nightmare, cosy in my bed. I peered down to see blood on my hands - in the woods.

Sanah Yaseen (13)

Prestwich Arts College, Manchester

THERE WAS ONCE A PARTY

Beautiful mansion filled with joyful people. Dancing, drinking, laughing, two explorers barge in past the locked doors. Flakes of dust fall from chandeliers. The woman says, 'Looks like nobody's been here for years!'
The man picks up a glass. Dust. There was once a party.

Rabiya Nazar (13)

Prestwich Arts College, Manchester

THE WIRES

Phoebe watched from behind the barrier. She craned her neck. Peering at the scene with an intense curiosity. She watched as her husband contemplated which wire to cut; red or blue. He shut his eyes tightly, cutting the red wire.
'Alright, cut!' yelled the director. 'That's all for today.'

Siân Popplewell (13)

Prestwich Arts College, Manchester

THE WOODS

We went for a stroll in the lush woods, I turned around to make sure Ellie was still there, she wasn't. I turned around and there was a strange, spooky house, Ellie was walking towards it. I chased after her. She entered the house, I followed her, the door slammed!

Chloe Kendall

Prestwich Arts College, Manchester

THE HAUNTING

Willow Street. The dead of night. A lot of strange things happened lately. Jennifer White couldn't sleep. Just then she heard a tortured moan. Terrified, she pulled the sheets over her head and squeezed her eyes shut. A cold breath sent a shiver down her spine. 'Die!' it whispered.

Joanna Rejmer (13)

Prestwich Arts College, Manchester

WAR!

Bright, orange, loud, near. I pass through the tunnel. Screams as people are engulfed by the flames. Red characters laughing menacingly. Yet at the end of the room all is calm, as a strange figure with a cloaked head, no face and scythes for arms sits and stares ... at me.

Connor Trenbath (13)

Prestwich Arts College, Manchester

BOMBS

Fire and burning buildings light the night. As the bombers pass, the noise draws out the screams of civilians in chaos and distress in the city below. The spotlight goes on and the anti-aircraft gunners get a glimpse of the shadowing planes above. For the survivors, Hell has arrived.

Alexander Moore (13)

St Aidan's RC Comprehensive School, Sunderland

AIRPORT

He was running very late! That was the last flight and he did not want to spend the night at the airport. He ran as fast as he could. There was only thirty minutes left. When he reached the gate his panic turned to a smile - his flight was delayed.

Ben Barker (12)

St Aidan's RC Comprehensive School, Sunderland

BOY SOLDIER

My heartbeat was increasing. Looking down on my sniper scope, glaring at my enemy, a Russian General, armed with a pistol. As I loaded my sniper rifle with a bullet, I pulled the trigger and I killed him. A bullet through his head, killed instantly.
A war had just started …

Timothy Ng (13)

St Aidan's RC Comprehensive School, Sunderland

THE DEATH OF SCHUMACHER

The racing cars were gone in an instant. Around the track they flew, tyres burning from the intensely hot burning track on a hot Brazilian day. All seemed to be going well, until, *smack!* Flames poured out from the car, Michael Schumacher was dead.
The movie made my spine shiver.

Louis Richardson (13)

St Aidan's RC Comprehensive School, Sunderland

TIME BOMB

John felt his heart beat in time with the beeping device he was perched over, both quickening with each moment. He held a knife tentatively over the maze of wires, picking out the one which his life was resting on. He carefully sliced through, and a single, final beep followed.

Michael Gibson (13)

St Aidan's RC Comprehensive School, Sunderland

RUN, RUN AS FAST AS YOU CAN

I sped away, racing as fast as I could. He was catching up. I needed to kick it up a notch, so I started darting around corners, desperate to escape from my pursuer. Through the back alleyway and the square. No sight of him. I knew I'd won the race.

Callum Bradfield (13)

St Aidan's RC Comprehensive School, Sunderland

THE DAWN OF DESTRUCTION

He looked around in horror to the state of the human devolution. What had the world become? He stood amongst the ghostly remnants of past society. Reminders of the thriving civilisation that was the human race. They were gone now. Only he was left. He knew his end was nigh ...

Jack Foley (13)

St Aidan's RC Comprehensive School, Sunderland

UNTITLED

One morning, I woke up. It was a sunny day but then I remembered it was Halloween. So I knew I had to go to the shops for a costume. Then Halloween was over before you knew it. I woke up the next morning and my family was murdered horribly.

Kristofer Venner (12)

St Aidan's RC Comprehensive School, Sunderland

FINALLY WORLD WAR 3

It finally came, World War Three. Every morning and night it was in and out. The false alarms went off, we had to rush to the bomb shelter and rush back in. 'I'm not doing that for nothing.'
That night the sirens spoke. Nobody moved. It was silent, too silent ...

Declan Swinhoe (13)

St Aidan's RC Comprehensive School, Sunderland

THE SHOOTOUT

Alejandro Cruz, the Mexican outlaw, now regretted that he didn't pay the blacksmith eighty dollars for that horse. The blacksmith stood sweating, focused on killing the outlaw. They both stood twenty steps apart, tense.
'Draw!'
Bang! Just one shot was fired.
A sombrero rolled along the floor. The outlaw dead.

Alex Hodgson

St Aidan's RC Comprehensive School, Sunderland

THE FINAL SHOT

There was me and him left on the battlefield. It was all down to one shot, whoever shot it was victorious. I was low on ammo and then I saw him. *Bang!* I missed. Then I was shot. There was green paint all over my shirt. We had lost.

Joseph Spencer (12)

St Aidan's RC Comprehensive School, Sunderland

THE HOUSE

The house next door is abandoned but every night there are noises like banging and shouting and creaking. One day I went to have a look. The house was all boarded up but there was a trapdoor. When I went inside there was a man with an axe ...

Kristian Donaldson (12)

St Aidan's RC Comprehensive School, Sunderland

PREDATOR

The monster was beneath its prey, aiming at its long neck. It was a fifty-metre, five hundred pounds of pure killing machine with its four large flippers. It powered at its prey, bit it on the neck, leaped out of the water. It fell back in, satisfied, very proud.

Brandon Lewis (12)

St Aidan's RC Comprehensive School, Sunderland

ZOMBIE LAND

I walked outside, there were loads of zombies, standing there hungry and horrible-looking. They looked at me, I got a bat and hit the zombies on the head, one by one they fell. Blood squirting, bones breaking, teeth shattering. I made it to the pub, then suddenly, *boom!*

Luke Applegarth (11)

St Aidan's RC Comprehensive School, Sunderland

IT ALL WENT WRONG

At last, performance night was here. We checked that we had everything. It was time to go. We set up our gear then Sir said, 'Nearly time boys.'
Just as Marcus was tuning up, *ping!* There went a guitar string, and guess what, yes, he didn't have any spares. *Help!*

Alexander Naylor Thubron (13)

St Aidan's RC Comprehensive School, Sunderland

STONE-COLD DELIVERY

He was in. He emptied out the dark brown fizzy liquid from the two-litre bottle and removed the package. He unwrapped the .22mm semi-automatic pistol and attached the silencer. 7 years training boiled down to this one night. His first 'assessment' as they liked to call it ...

James Duncan (13)

St Aidan's RC Comprehensive School, Sunderland

50 YEARS LATER

Area five, it was nothing but a rats' home after the nuclear war. The consternation of one man standing there. The only man alive, two eyes, one nose, one mouth. He was a human, how did he survive? A troglodyte of nature, important people promised the truth. Important people lie.

Joseph Anderson (13)

St Aidan's RC Comprehensive School, Sunderland

UNTITLED

I darted over the hill in desperation, the speeding bullets shooting past me. Blood-red splatters covered me from a man wounded. I ran across the cold, dark field shouting, 'I'm out of paint balls.'

Adrian Lindsay (13)

St Aidan's RC Comprehensive School, Sunderland

A WESTERN TALE

Whilst in the hustle and bustle of the town I headed for the saloon, the wind was getting fierce now. I entered the old squeaky door, the music of the piano came to a halt, as if I had become deaf on the spot.
'I need a drink, right now.'

Liam Hall (13)

St Aidan's RC Comprehensive School, Sunderland

MINI SAGAS - CREATIVE CAPERS - TALES FROM THE NORTH

THE ASSAULT

One day, I was walking down the street, when suddenly, Britain's most wanted jumped out of a back-alley and thrust a machete into my side and knocked me onto the floor.

With all my strength I hurled myself on top of him and called 999 with my phone … Arrested.

Matthew John Baister (12)

St Aidan's RC Comprehensive School, Sunderland

THE ANT AND THE BIRD

I am an adventurer. An ant is running up the tree. A baby bird sees the ant and starts chasing the ant. The ant runs very fast. The bird is faster and he eats the ant. The ant is falling through the black hole of the bird's neck and dies.

Daniel David Simpson (12)

St Aidan's RC Comprehensive School, Sunderland

A TOUR OF DUTY

As they ran, suddenly they were ambushed in the desert whilst dying of thirst. Their shots were getting less accurate. Then one of the sergeants took one shot and luckily got him. On the way back to base they didn't encounter anyone else.

Daniel Matthew Forrest (13)

St Aidan's RC Comprehensive School, Sunderland

UNTITLED

The lights went out and the roar of the V8 engines charged down to the corner. Gary's car was getting hit. He managed to get round the first corner. As he was accelerating, disaster struck ... The number 7 car hit him. 'Mam, this game you got me is really awful.'

Matthew Thomas (13)

St Aidan's RC Comprehensive School, Sunderland

TIME STOPS

I was in the time machine. First stop, Jurassic. I opened the door and was hit by the stale stench of a T-rex. Next stop, Tudor times. I opened the door, 'Off with his head.' I quickly got back into the machine. I opened the door and ... 'I'm not amused.'

Spencer John Thomas Hardy (12)

St Aidan's RC Comprehensive School, Sunderland

THE DEADLY HOUND

Accelerating through the woods, a vicious hound snarling, getting closer. Suddenly, the man stumbled and fell, the hound gained ground, growling and grinning. The man turned, trying to get up and get away. The roots grabbing his legs. He had no strength to get up. The hound leapt onto him.

Benjamin Mark Weighill (12)

St Aidan's RC Comprehensive School, Sunderland

SHADOWS BE GONE

He drew his sword. *Slash!* The shadow dropped to the floor. Suddenly, he was surrounded by darkness as he ran for his life. He turned and watched the darkness close in on him. Then the darkness fled from its enemy … The sun had returned.

Louis Simpson (13)

St Aidan's RC Comprehensive School, Sunderland

A STUPID DOG

A cat strolls along the wall, a dog sitting getting a tan, looking at the sky above. When the cat crosses his view, he pounces and lands on the road. He lays there whilst the cat watches … then *bang!* The dog is hit by a car at 40mph and dies.

James George Taylor (12)

St Aidan's RC Comprehensive School, Sunderland

SEA SPRAY

The ship rumbled and creaked, water pounded the sides. The men stumbled across the ship, then lightning struck a crew member. It was as if God was against me. Some of the men jumped in the water, then the ship creaked and sank.

Charlie O'Hagan (13)

St Aidan's RC Comprehensive School, Sunderland

EVACUATION FROM CITY 17

The evacuation site was just past the mall. Suddenly, there was a flash of light as army rangers poured out of the mall. They were being chased by something big. Helicopters and rangers were being thrown through the air as the intruder moved closer. I thought there was no hope.

Shaun Hunt (13)

St Aidan's RC Comprehensive School, Sunderland

FINDING THE TRUTH

There's a heart-racing military chase for a young man. The person has experimental DNA. He sprints into a Sunderland station. The man explodes, 'This is too dangerous for mankind!' The man throws the cube to the floor, now lives of many more are in huge and definite jeopardy.

Liam Moir (13)

St Aidan's RC Comprehensive School, Sunderland

PHILLIP AND THE PIGS

Phillip witnessed the wolf panting and punching the pigs' house. He darted at it. One fatal blow knocked out the wolf; accordingly asking the pigs for tea. After, he thought to himself, *nobody speaks 'wolf' so nobody knew it was warning them.* With that remark he wore his butcher's hat.

Tyler Clark (13)

St Aidan's RC Comprehensive School, Sunderland

THE CHASE

I hesitated, panting as I glanced over my shoulder at the pursuers. They were closing in on me now. I tried to hurry, my fur coat heavy under the intense sunlight. They surrounded me, towering over me.
She spoke, 'Come on Lucky, hurry. It's time to go to the vets!'

Christopher Byers (13)

St Aidan's RC Comprehensive School, Sunderland

RUMBLE

R*umble,* his stomach churned as the hunger had eventually got to him. He could not take the pain anymore, his lips dripping at just the thought. *Chomp, chomp,* he began to eat, digging in as if he was a vulture.

Keeran Harrison (13)

St Aidan's RC Comprehensive School, Sunderland

THE LION AND THE ZEBRA

The zebra was in a horrific position, scattering away from the galloping lion. The scenes and the lion were in a terrible state. The dazzling lion took a massive leap towards the zebra. Flying in the air, the lion's claws came out five inches. And then, *bang, clatter, clatter, clatter.*

Cerian Anthony Young (13)

St Aidan's RC Comprehensive School, Sunderland

THIEF ALERT!

He walked in cunningly and went up the aisle, but the walk felt like a mile. The boy then took chase with sweat on his face and disappeared quickly like it was a race.

Sam Hildreth (12)

St Aidan's RC Comprehensive School, Sunderland

DRENCHED IN GUNFIRE

The loud noise of gunfire surrounded me, my friends were all dead. I was the last alive, then I was hit. I fell to the ground, drenched. There was no hope. Then, 'Kids c'mon, the tea's ready - put the water guns down!'

Jack Bailey (12)

St Aidan's RC Comprehensive School, Sunderland

AN ENCOUNTER WITH DEATH

I crept into the room, the stench was foul. A shiver crept down my spine. I was close. I grabbed my equipment. I was there, staring death in the eye. They gave me the disgusting substance and told me to sit down and try it.

Yuck! School dinners are disgusting.

Cameron Bevan (12)

St Aidan's RC Comprehensive School, Sunderland

THE DAY OF THE EGG

As I sat there watching my brothers sizzle and burn, in my cardboard ship, my life flashed before my eyes. That second I was picked up and as my hard shell broke I burned in the frying pan. The last thing I saw was the gleaming trident of the Devil.

Jack Fletcher (12)

St Aidan's RC Comprehensive School, Sunderland

PREDATOR AND PREY

I was running through the forest but something moved, like a mouse scuffling on old dry leaves. Suddenly, it got louder. Then, like someone running, it echoed all around. So I stopped and turned. Then the noise stopped. *Crash!* Something had happened behind me. I turned. *Bang!* I dropped dead.

Joshua Cox (12)

St Aidan's RC Comprehensive School, Sunderland

THE TERROR

Jim was frightened in his bed, sick with fear building inside him, nearly crying. Something scary rattled under his bed, he knew I was there but he was still trembling. The voice of the monster echoed through the room saying in a deep scary voice, 'It's Monday tomorrow, ha, ha!'

Liam Ralston (12)

St Aidan's RC Comprehensive School, Sunderland

UNTITLED

Dan the dog was bored of the airport and wanted some attention from his keeper. When he turned around his keeper was talking to a man. Dan whined to get attention. He was ignored. Dan barked, nudging the man's bag. He was arrested. *All in a day's work,* thought Dan.

Adam Wilson (12)

St Aidan's RC Comprehensive School, Sunderland

THE FINAL

It was the ninetieth minute of the World Cup final, England V Spain.

Rooney was through! Rooney was face-to-face with the Spanish keeper, he stumbled right and scooped the ball over the keeper's head. The ball slowly rolled over the line … then suddenly there was a massive cheer!

Jack Wilson (12)

St Aidan's RC Comprehensive School, Sunderland

EVERY PUPIL'S NIGHTMARE

Everybody shook with fear. Pale white faces showed all around the room. The time was coming. Some passed out, some were sick, some hung their heads. I gripped my seat hard, the pressure was getting to me.

A big scary lady walked to the front. 'Right children, your SATs begin!'

Christopher McGill (12)

St Aidan's RC Comprehensive School, Sunderland

UNTITLED

John looked up at the fearless killer. You could see the fear in his eyes. You could see some old boots of a previous victim he had murdered before. That is when he saw the gun. He tried to escape through the ajar door. But it was too late. *Bang!*

Philip Wilson (13)

St Aidan's RC Comprehensive School, Sunderland

DOGFIGHT

The German pilot was flying high over England when hot lead slammed into his left wing. The Spitfire was behind him. He barrel-rolled to get away. The other plane was more nimble. He was alone and getting shot at.
Then the pilot woke up, it was just a dream.

Ryan Hall (14)

St Aidan's RC Comprehensive School, Sunderland

UNTITLED

As I stood and watched the beast tear and shred the meat off the deer, the lion looked at me with blood slowly dripping off its mouth and roared. I looked into the lion's eyes and I saw its prey, it was another deer. The lion crept towards it.

John Marsh (14)

St Aidan's RC Comprehensive School, Sunderland

THE WANTED

The criminal raced through the back-alleys. He sprinted for his life. The police were desperate to catch the criminal because he had committed desperate robberies to feed his family.
Bang! The police had shot him in the back of the leg. Blood splurted everywhere. He was down and out.

Elliot Tench (13)

St Aidan's RC Comprehensive School, Sunderland

THE MARATHON

The race started, he sprinted and dodged, the runner was in a race with the champion and he was determined to finish and win.

Crash! One of the runners fell out, the champion was still behind him. The runner had a last burst of energy. The last corner came and ...

Harry Richardson (14)

St Aidan's RC Comprehensive School, Sunderland

THE RUN DOWN

They stopped, looked, but saw nothing. The race had begun. The sound of the crunching of branches and leaves emerged from the woods. They kept walking ... the sounds of horses came near, then the slicing of meat came upon them. Blood splattered on the edge of their blades, then silence.

Troy Henderson (14)

St Aidan's RC Comprehensive School, Sunderland

THE CHOICES WE TAKE

As I walked into the store, I pondered, which poor animal I should liberate. All the poor creatures, rejected in life, and I had the chance to change one's life, it made me sad and my throat … stained with guilt croaked out, 'That one.' The owner … drowned himself in ecstasy.

Jack Andrew Hunter

St Aidan's RC Comprehensive School, Sunderland

THE SHOOTING STARS

It shot across the sky like a bullet out of a gun, as I shouted, 'Close your eyes and make a wish.' It was like a shining majestic horse galloping across the sky. Then just like that it was gone and we all stared into the path of the star.

Christopher Dewart (14)

St Aidan's RC Comprehensive School, Sunderland

UNTITLED

Me and three friends decided to go fishing one day at Seaburn pier. We were all having a good time when suddenly a strong wind emerged, the waves started to pound the pier and water splashed over the side. I thought I was dead, but then I remembered the barriers.

Lewis Meldrum (13)

St Aidan's RC Comprehensive School, Sunderland

THE ALLEY

I turned round, it was there in the dark, cold and damp alley. Its slender and tall posture and long stick-armed body was approaching me, for every step it moved I took two steps back. Suddenly, it got distracted and scurried away as the council worker swept the streets.

Jordan Pattison (13)

St Aidan's RC Comprehensive School, Sunderland

UNTITLED

Pack of tigers prowling around the jungle, waiting to see their tea. They stop, look, listen to see zebras trotting past. The tigers pounce and strike, they sink their teeth into the zebra's neck to see the blood squirt out. They tear the meat out of its body. Yum-yum.

Clayton Atkinson (14)

St Aidan's RC Comprehensive School, Sunderland

WAR'S A BEACH

Bryan ran along the lines of battle, bullets were flying and he watched as friends died like dogs. As he advanced down the beach his friend was shot. As he approached his cold, dead body he tripped on a landmine. It exploded in a bang and then he died.

Connor Richmond (14)

St Aidan's RC Comprehensive School, Sunderland

THE FOOTBALL GAME

'Help!' a girl shouted.

I turned around, no one was there. I ran down the street and saw nothing until a giant hairy troll came out of nowhere. I turned and ran quickly, he was chasing me. I turned down a back-alley, I heard a big bang.

Kieron Martin (14)

St Aidan's RC Comprehensive School, Sunderland

UNTITLED

A car screeched around the corner, travelling about 80mph. As it pulled out of oversteer, the police were behind, like a hunter after its prey. The car was a Mercedes-AMG, it passed me. I looked into the driver's eyes for a second, I realised who it was, it was …

Nathanieal Brettle (14)

St Aidan's RC Comprehensive School, Sunderland

BLINDED

Lights blinding my eyes, it was then the feeling struck me. I'd been here before. I'd taken the chance to step unnervingly onto the tracks and gingerly cover my eyes from those beaming headlights. My life flashed before me, but this time it wasn't a dream, the train wouldn't stop.

Lindsey Shepherd (14)

Shavington High School, Crewe

THE TEST

A dazzling, harsh glare stung my feeble eyes. Around me, was eternal blackness, oozing from every corner; swallowing my insubstantial endeavour to scream, 'No!' I struggled backwards; my attempts wasted - the blazing glow burnt and tore apart my eyes like a laser …
'No, Ellen dear, you won't be needing glasses.'

Ellen Thompson (13)

Shavington High School, Crewe

THE STARE

The lifeless glare drove straight through him; burning his lungs as it did. Unable to move, he tried to call out but no sound came. Fear was stealing his life away. He broke and darted this way and that but it kept following. He stopped. The feline turned and ran.

Jacques Cador (14)

Shavington High School, Crewe

BEATEN

Battered, bruised. I stood there, hopelessly watching it being pummelled beyond belief. What could I do? Nothing. The amount of violence was astonishing! I don't know why I came here. I shouldn't let people talk me into this kind of brutality ... I suppose it's only a punch bag. I'll live.

Ben Hallam (14)

Shavington High School, Crewe

PLUNGED

I flung my swimming trunks on, slowly. My warm feet touched the icy, bitter water. Straight ahead of me was a huge grey thing lurking in the distance. It seemed to approach me. Shivering, I climbed the steep steps - *splash!* I did it, I dived off the steel board.

Jonathan Tyrer (13)

Shavington High School, Crewe

FALLING

Floating above the mountains, above the abyss, mist hanging on the trees, rolling water moving over the rocks. Dew-entwined grass rocking gently in the wind. All quiet, peaceful. I'm sweeping, falling as graceful as a bird. I pull, desperate. The world's bigger now. It looks like time. Goodbye. Forever …

Jack Stokes (14)

Shavington High School, Crewe

THREE LIONS

The ball leaves his boot, heading for goal. It dips and swerves. The goalkeeper scrambles across the goal-line. Hearts in mouths. Nails bitten to the core. The vuvuzelas pause, you could hear a pin drop. The net bulges, could it be the goal that wins England the World Cup?

Kieran Barker (14)

Shavington High School, Crewe

SILENCE

Swerving around the men! Clenching my disfigured arm. The torment of the bullet crippled my arm. Men were falling around me, this was war, this was murder! Suddenly, a pain struck my lower back. Agony ripped through every nerve and muscle in my body. An eerie blackness fell. Death. Silence!

Daniel Embley (13)

Shavington High School, Crewe

A MONOPOLY STORY

Scottie paced silently around his cell. He had tried almost everything to escape: turning on the waterworks and taking several chances, but nothing worked. His house, recently extended on Mayfair, made him bankrupt and eleven words haunted his subconscious … 'Go to jail, do not pass go, do not collect £200.'

Katherine Blumer (14)

Shavington High School, Crewe

THE ZONE

Always hunting, always killing. Scanning the obliterated ruins of the battlefield. All I see are pawns of death, all seeking eternal glory written in the spilt blood of others. But only one can forever be printed in glory; forever remembered in the hearts of others. Another soul lost.

James Ward (14)

Shavington High School, Crewe

AWAKE

It was dark when I woke up. Not everyone was awake. Dad was. So was Mum. Every morning Dad is the first awake, no matter what! There's this place, Earth. Things that watch us. Watch us sparkle. Glow. Live. It's interesting watching them. Especially from here. Up in the sky.

Ella Davies (14)

Shavington High School, Crewe

PAVEMENT

Here I am once again. All alone I sit here, looking up at the suspenseful world around me. They just walk all over me, not a care in the world for my tender feelings. People don't even look at me, no acknowledgement of my existence. They even spit at me.

Caitlin Hill (14)

Shavington High School, Crewe

BETRAYED

Simon and his pet chicken, Henry, were best friends! Actually that was Simon's only friend.

One night, Simon visited KFC. When he returned home, Simon rushed to his room where he had left Henry. But in place of the beloved chicken was a bloodstained feather and note: 'You killed me'.

Heather Morley (14)

Shavington High School, Crewe

CUTTING IT FINE

The whining noise flew past, just millimeters from my ear. There it went again, skimming across my head. I tried to get away, but if I moved out of the chair, I knew it'd have my head off.

'There you are, number two back and sides. That's five pounds please.'

Jacob O'Neill (13)

Shavington High School, Crewe

BLAST OFF!

The time until departure is drawing ever closer. My metallic, bulging suit makes every stride feel like a mile, as I quickly clamber to my position. The strenuous hours, endless preparation, all come down to this moment. My adventure. The day I fly into space! Five … four … three … two … *one!*

Claire Madeley (14)

Shavington High School, Crewe

PREDATOR

Soaring through the air, its feathers fluttered as the wind went whistling past. Zooming on its prey, its head gleamed as it appeared out of the sun's gaze. Swooping downwards to the sea of men the swarm blackened out the light … In darkness men screamed as the arrows penetrated them.

Sam Klein (14)

Shavington High School, Crewe

JACK

Jack had a black eye. It happened that morning. Jack was meeting with young and beautiful Jamie for coffee. Jack asked her whether she had any kids. Jamie mentioned that she was a proud mum of two kids. Jack added, 'So are you married?' and Jack had a black eye.

Callum Powell (14)

Shavington High School, Crewe

EATEN

Its round, petrifying stare administered the most unholy pain imaginable. The feeling of your soul being ripped from the very marrow of your body. Such an unfortunate tragedy, a creature so very humble. Yet this curse it carries. The poor, lonely, gummy bear.
'Oh well, at least you taste nice.'

Josh Wainwright (14)

Shavington High School, Crewe

SMASHED

He sat there with his friends. Who would get picked? It was him. He was taken out of the cold room and across to the big bowl. He watched as his friends had their sides smashed open. It was his turn. 'Well, not all eggs get to be in cakes.'

Jonty George (14)

Shavington High School, Crewe

SACRIFICE

Love ... a dangerous thing. As Jessie raced around the corner, she realised it would cost her her life. He was already there. Her only purpose for living. And yet the only reason she now threw herself in front of the fatal bullet speeding towards him ... love. It tears us apart.

Faith Whittaker (13)

Shavington High School, Crewe

DON'T STOP

He saw his face, that stare of evil. He reached into his pocket, removing the gun. His life played back, remembering the day he arrested him. Still unable to move. The flash blinded him as the bullet struck him with great force. He crashed down, while the man staggered away!

Thomas Beswick (13)

Shavington High School, Crewe

THE MIDNIGHT MANSION

The lights suddenly flickered back on. Sandy found her hand reached out, about to open the door from which the deafening scream had come from. Gently pushing the door, another scream occurred and it went pitch-black.

'Alice, why are your Halloween stories so scary?' cried Sandy, running inside.

Kate Arnott (14)

Shavington High School, Crewe

THE NEW KING

Arthas lay down his sword, Frostmourne, after massacring the thousand protecting the fallen king of Azaroth, and took his place atop the throne of Stormwind keep. 'Richard!' yelled a voice from the kitchen. 'Your dinner's ready.'
Richard turned his computer off. 'Awesome, bangers and mash!'

Luke Worgan (14)
Shavington High School, Crewe

YOUNG WRITERS INFORMATION

We hope you have enjoyed reading this book - and that you will continue to enjoy it in the coming years.

If you like reading and creative writing drop us a line, or give us a call, and we'll send you a free information pack.

Alternatively if you would like to order further copies of this book or any of our other titles, then please give us a call or log onto our website at **www.youngwriters.co.uk**

Young Writers Information
Remus House
Coltsfoot Drive
Peterborough
PE2 9JX
Tel: (01733) 890066